Catch that Hat!

First published in 2010
by Wayland

Text copyright © Andy Blackford
Illustration copyright © Richard Watson

Wayland
338 Euston Road
London NW1 3BH

Wayland Australia
Level 17/207 Kent Street
Sydney, NSW 2000

Series Editor: Louise John
Cover design: Paul Cherrill
Design: D.R.ink
Consultant: Shirley Bickler

A CIP catalogue record for this book is available from the British Library.

ISBN 9780750262156

Printed in China

Wayland is a division of Hachette Children's Books,
an Hachette UK Company

www.hachette.co.uk

Catch that Hat!

Written by Andy Blackford
Illustrated by Richard Watson

WAYLAND

It was a windy day.
Ruby went for a walk
with her dog, Merlin.

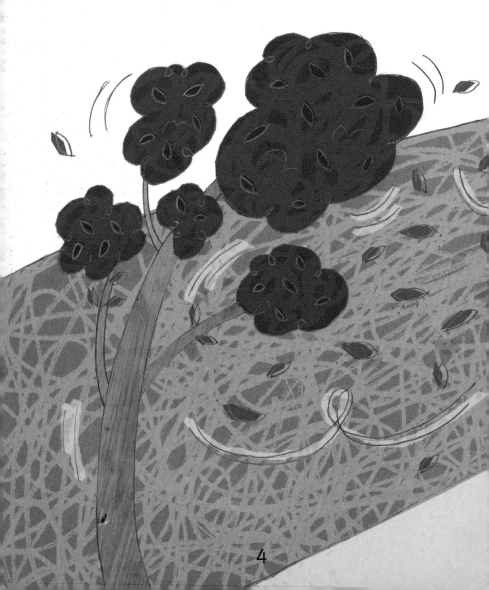

4

The wind was strong. It whooshed down the street and swished in the trees.

Then the wind grabbed
Mr Murray's hat and
blew it away!

"Catch that hat!" cried
Mr Murray. Merlin chased
after it. So did Ruby.

Now the wind was getting stronger. It howled like a wolf.

It blew a tile off the roof. CRASH!

"It's lucky that it didn't hit anyone!" said Ruby.

The wind was getting
stronger. Now it roared
like a lion!

It blew a tree down behind
Ruby and Merlin. CRASH!

"It's lucky that it didn't hit anyone!" said Ruby.

Still they did not catch that hat. But they did stop an old lady from blowing away.

Ruby and Merlin chased
the hat to the beach.
A big wave landed just
behind them. SPLASH!

"THAT was lucky!" said Ruby.

The wind grabbed the hat again, but Merlin jumped up and got it.

"Well done, Merlin!"
said Ruby.

Soon, the wind stopped. Ruby and Merlin walked back past the tree, past the tile and past the old lady.

"The wind has made a big mess!" said Ruby.

Merlin gave Mr Murray his hat back.

"Thank you!" said Mr Murray,
and he gave Merlin a biscuit.

"Hold on to your hat,
Mr Murray!" said Ruby.

START READING is a series of highly enjoyable books for beginner readers. **The books have been carefully graded to match the Book Bands widely used in schools.** This enables readers to be sure they choose books that match their own reading ability.

Look out for the Band colour on the book in our Start Reading logo.

The Bands are:

Pink Band 1A & 1B

Red Band 2

Yellow Band 3

Blue Band 4

Green Band 5

Orange Band 6

Turquoise Band 7

Purple Band 8

Gold Band 9

START READING books can be read independently or shared with an adult. They promote the enjoyment of reading through satisfying stories supported by fun illustrations.

Andy Blackford used to play guitar in a rock band. Besides books, he writes about running and scuba diving. He has run across the Sahara Desert and dived with tiger sharks. He lives in the country with his wife and daughter, a friendly collie dog and a grumpy cat.

Richard Watson was born in 1980 and from as soon as he was able to read and write, he always had his nose in a book and a pen in his hand. After school, Richard went on to study illustration in Lincoln and graduated in 2003. He has worked as an illustrator ever since.